Poké Rap

I want to be the very best the[re]
To beat all the rest, yeah, that's my cause

Catch 'em, Catch 'em, Gotta catch 'em all

Pokémon I'll search across the land
Look far and wide
Release from my hand
The power that's inside

Catch 'em, Catch 'em, Gotta catch 'em all
Pokémon!

Gotta catch 'em all, Gotta catch 'em all
Gotta catch 'em all, Gotta catch 'em all

At least one hundred and fifty or more to see
To be a Pokémon Master is my destiny

Catch 'em, Catch 'em, Gotta catch 'em all
Gotta catch 'em all, Pokémon! (repeat three times)

Can YOU Rap all 150?

**Here's more of the Poké Rap.
Catch book #9
Journey to the Orange Islands
for the next 32 Pokémon!**

Articuno, Jynx, Nidorina, Beedrill
Haunter, Squirtle, Chansey
Parasect, Exeggcute, Muk, Dewgong
Pidgeotto, Lapras, Vulpix, Rhydon

Charizard, Machamp, Pinsir, Koffing
Dugtrio, Golbat, Staryu, Magikarp
Ninetales, Ekans, Omastar
Scyther, Tentacool, Dragonair, Magmar

Words and Music by Tamara Loeffler and John Siegler
Copyright © 1999 Pikachu Music (BMI)
Worldwide rights for Pikachu Music administered by Cherry River Music Co. (BMI)
All Rights Reserved   Used by Permission

D0338132

There are more books
about Pokémon.

Collect them all!

coming soon

*Three Exciting New Adventures
about the Orange Islands*

POKéMON™

Return of the Squirtle Squad

Adapted by Tracey West

SCHOLASTIC INC.
New York   Toronto   London   Auckland   Sydney
Mexico City   New Delhi   Hong Kong

ISBN 0-439-15429-4

©1995, 1996, 1998 Nintendo, CREATURES, GAME FREAK.
TM & ® are trademarks of Nintendo.
© 2000 Nintendo.

All rights reserved. Published by Scholastic Inc.
SCHOLASTIC and associated logos are trademarks
and/or registered trademarks of Scholastic Inc.

12   11   10   9   8   7   6   7 8 9 10/0

Printed in the U.S.A.

First Scholastic printing, April 2000

The World of Pokémon

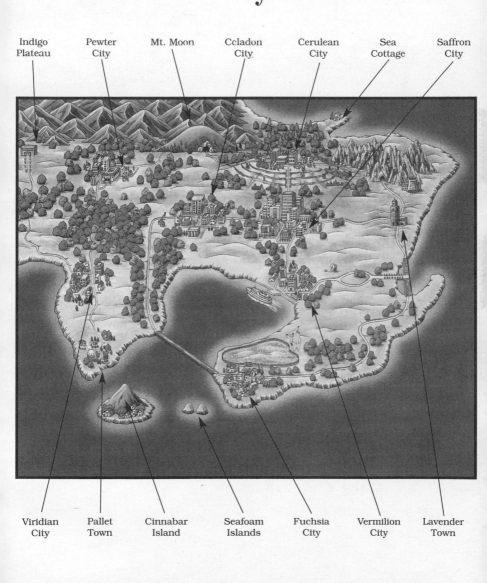

Indigo Plateau • Pewter City • Mt. Moon • Celadon City • Cerulean City • Sea Cottage • Saffron City

Viridian City • Pallet Town • Cinnabar Island • Seafoam Islands • Fuchsia City • Vermilion City • Lavender Town

Pikachu Peekaboo Contest

Win Pokémon prizes!

This Pikachu is hiding throughout the book.

Count the number of times you find Pikachu in this pose as you read. Then check out the official rules in the back of the book for all the details.

Gotta Find 'em All!

Squirtle Strikes Again!

"Searching for wild Pokémon sure is exhausting," Ash Ketchum said. The ten-year-old boy took his knapsack off his back. He wearily sank down in the grass.

"This does look like a good place to stop for a rest," his friend Misty agreed.

Ash looked around. Shady trees lined the trail where they were hiking. A bubbling stream flowed nearby.

"Our Pokémon could use a break, too," said Ash's friend Brock. He took a red-and-white Poké Ball from his knapsack and opened it. Vulpix, a Pokémon that looked like a fox, appeared. Next came Geodude, a Rock Pokémon with two strong arms.

Vulpix and Geodude ran off to play with Pikachu, Ash's Electric Pokémon. Pikachu looked like a yellow mouse.

"Good idea," Misty said. She let out her Psyduck, a Water Pokémon. Then she set down Togepi, a tiny Pokémon that still wore the colorful eggshell it had hatched from.

Ash let Bulbasaur and Squirtle out of their Poké Balls. Bulbasaur looked like a dinosaur with a plant bulb on its back. Squirtle looked like a turtle.

Ash leaned back against his knapsack and smiled. Catching and raising Pokémon was hard work. He had been on the road

for months, trying to learn how to train these amazing creatures so he could become a Pokémon Master. Sometimes being a Pokémon trainer was dangerous. He'd even been hurt a few times. But spending peaceful times like this with his Pokémon made it all worthwhile.

Ash stood up and stretched. "I feel pretty grimy. I think I'll go wash off in that stream," he said.

Ash trudged off the path and climbed down the stream's bank. He knelt down and dipped his hands into the stream.

Suddenly, a blast of cold water hit him in the face.

"Hey!" Ash shouted.

"Squirtle squirtle squirtle!"

Ash wiped the water from his eyes. Squirtle was standing in the stream, laughing hard.

The Pokémon had used its Water Gun Attack to squirt water at Ash!

"Very funny," Ash muttered. He climbed back up the bank and walked over to Misty and Brock.

"Looks like Squirtle got you!" Misty giggled.

"That Pokémon prankster drives me crazy sometimes," Ash complained.

"Maybe," Brock said. "But don't forget, Squirtle's always been there when you needed it."

"That's right," Misty said. "Squirtle's one of your best Pokémon."

Ash took a towel from his knapsack and dried off. He knew Misty and Brock were right.

Ash stretched out in the grass and closed his eyes. He started to think about all the times Squirtle had helped him out.

It all started when they first met. . . .

2

The Squirtle Squad

Ash met Squirtle early on his Pokémon journey. It was a sunny day, and he, Misty, Brock, and Pikachu were walking down a dirt path on their way to the next town.

Ash stopped, startled, as his foot sank into the ground. He turned to warn his friends, but he was too late. The loose dirt gave way underneath them. They all plummeted into a pit!

"Ouch!" Ash cried as he landed with a thud. He climbed to his feet.

"Is everyone all right?" Ash asked.

"*Pika,*" Pikachu replied. Brock and Misty nodded.

"This must be some kind of prank," Brock guessed.

"Someone has a bad sense of humor," Misty said angrily.

Ash agreed. "Who'd play such a rotten trick?"

The sound of laughter answered him. Ash looked up. Five Squirtle Pokémon were looking down at them and laughing. But they didn't look like ordinary Squirtle. They wore dark sunglasses.

"What's so funny?" Misty yelled. "We could have been hurt!"

"Dangerous practical jokes are nothing to laugh about," Ash added.

The group of Squirtle laughed even harder.

Ash was really angry now. He climbed out of the pit. Then he pulled out Pikachu. Misty and Brock climbed out, too.

The five Squirtle were lined up, facing them. Ash noticed that one Squirtle in the center seemed to be their leader. Its sunglasses had pointy frames, while the others wore round sunglasses.

Ash took out Dexter, his Pokédex. Dexter contained computer files with information about every known Pokémon.

"Squirtle," said the handheld computer. "This tiny turtle Pokémon draws its long neck into its shell to launch incredible water attacks with amazing range and accuracy. The blasts can be quite powerful."

"Wow!" Ash said. "It would be great to capture my very own Squirtle. Pikachu, go!"

Pikachu nodded, then ran toward the gang of Squirtle. It aimed an electric charge at the Squirtle leader. But one of the other Squirtle jumped in front of the blast. It absorbed the shock, then fell to the ground, weakened.

The Squirtle leader frowned. It stepped forward and faced Pikachu.

"*Squirtle!*" it said in a low, threatening voice.

"*Pika!*" Pikachu replied.

Ash tensed. It looked like a Pokémon battle was about to begin.

Then the sound of a siren filled the air. The siren sound got closer.

The Squirtle leader got a panicked look on its face. It turned to the other Squirtle.

"Squirtle! Squirtle!" it said urgently.

All five Squirtle ran off, leaving a cloud of dust behind them.

A police officer on a motorcycle pulled up next to Ash. Ash knew from his travels that the blue-haired officer was named Jenny. There was an officer named Jenny in each town he visited. They all looked alike and had the same name.

"Are you guys all right?" Officer Jenny

asked. "Has anyone been hurt?"

"We're fine," Ash said. "Who were those Pokémon?"

"That Pokémon gang calls itself the Squirtle Squad," Jenny explained. "They're all Squirtle who were abandoned by their Pokémon trainers. So now they run wild and play tricks on the whole town."

"Deserted by their trainers," Ash said. "That's pretty sad."

Jenny nodded. "If they had somebody to care about them, they wouldn't have turned out to be as bad as they are."

Ash looked down the road after them.

"I guess I feel kind of sorry for them," Ash said. "But I still hope we never run into them again!"

3

Team Rocket's Trick

While Ash and his friends talked to Officer Jenny, the Squirtle Squad was getting into even more trouble.

The squad was spying on two humans and a Pokémon. One of the humans was a teenage girl with long, red hair. The other was a boy with purple hair. The Pokémon was a Meowth, a white Pokémon that looked like a cat.

It was Team Rocket, a notorious trio of Pokémon thieves. Team Rocket was always trying to steal rare Pokémon, especially Ash's Pikachu.

But the Squirtle Squad didn't know about that. And they didn't care. All they cared about was the delicious picnic lunch Team Rocket was about to eat.

The Squirtle leader stepped out from behind its hiding place. The other Squirtle followed.

"Squirtle squirtle!" the leader told Jessie and James, the two humans.

"Meowth, what's it saying?" James asked.

Meowth could speak human language, and knew the language of most Pokémon as well.

"I think it said, 'Give us your food—or else!'" Meowth translated.

Jessie looked shocked. "You're threatening us?" she snapped at the squad leader. "We're Team Rocket. We do the threatening around here."

"Squirtle squirtle!" the leader said angrily.

"Let's show these little creeps," Jessie said.

"I'm game," James said.

Jessie and James took out their Poké

Balls and stepped forward to battle the Squirtle Squad . . .

. . . and fell right into a Squirtle Squad trap!

The Squirtle Squad laughed. Jessie, James, and Meowth had landed in a heap at the bottom of a pit. The Squirtle leader barked out commands, and in no time Team Rocket was tied up and the squad was gobbling their lunch.

"They're eating all the jelly donuts!" Jessie cried.

"They're drinking all the lemonade," James moaned.

"This is cruel and unusual!" wailed Meowth.

The Squirtle Squad ignored them. They started on a pile of peanut-butter-and-jelly sandwiches.

Jessie looked thoughtful for a minute. Then she spoke.

"Hey, Squirtle," she said in her smoothest voice. "How'd you like to do a little job for us?"

The Squirtle Squad stopped eating and looked up.

"There are these three kids with a Pikachu," Jessie continued. "Our boss would be most appreciative if you helped us capture them. He'd make it worth your while — if you know what I mean."

"Squirtle squirtle!" the leader snapped.

"The Squirtle said, 'Forget it. We know humans can't be trusted,'" Meowth translated.

"So make them trust us," James pleaded.

"Leave it to me," Meowth said. "I have an idea."

Meowth faced the Squirtle Squad.

"These two humans are my pets," Meowth told them. "I trained them. They're not very smart."

The Squirtle leader looked curious.

"What are you talking about, you ungrateful —" James began, but Meowth kicked him in the shins.

"Don't ever raise your voice to me again, you bad human!" Meowth yelled. "Bad, bad human!"

The Squirtle Squad laughed. They untied Meowth.

"See, you guys can trust me," Meowth said.

"Squirtle squirtle!" said the leader.

"This is ridiculous," Jessie muttered.

"And painful," James groaned, thinking about his shins.

"But it's working," Meowth said. "They trust me now."

Meowth turned to the Squirtle leader. "So what do you say? Will you help us capture Pikachu?"

16

"*Squirtle!*" The Squirtle leader nodded. It untied Jessie and James.

"Brilliant move," Jessie whispercd to Meowth. "With the Squirtle Squad on our side, Pikachu will be ours!"

Save Pikachu!

"I think I caught something!" Misty said. She felt a tug on her fishing line.

Ash and his friends needed a rest after their encounter with the Squirtle Squad. They were sitting on a grassy riverbank.

Misty pulled on her fishing pole.

"I've caught one!" she cried.

But instead of a fish on the line, a Squirtle popped out of the water. It shot a blast of water out of its mouth, soaking Misty, Ash, Brock, and Pikachu.

Ash brushed his wet hair out of his eyes.

"That's it!" he yelled. "I've had enough of your pranks, Squirtle Squad."

The Squirtle jumped out of the water and onto the riverbank.

"Pikachu, battle that Squirtle!" Ash ordered.

"Pika!" Pikachu said. Its cheeks glimmered with electric sparks. That always happened before Pikachu made an Electric Attack.

But Pikachu didn't have time. The Squirtle retracted into its shell. The shell began to spin around and around like a

wheel. It flew through the air, right at Pikachu.

Bam! The spinning shell knocked Pikachu into the river.

Pikachu was dazed, but was able to swim. It started to paddle back to shore.

Then another Pokémon appeared in the river. It wasn't a Squirtle. It was an orange Water Pokémon with a horn on its head.

"It's a Goldeen!" Misty shouted. "Pikachu, watch out for its horn!"

It was too late. The Goldeen was a faster swimmer than Pikachu, and it quickly caught up. Goldeen's horn smacked into Pikachu with a sickening thud.

Pikachu flew out of the water and landed with a crash on the riverbank. Its eyes were closed.

Pikachu was knocked out!

"Pikachu! No!" Ash cried. He ran to help Pikachu. Brock and Misty ran to Pikachu's side, too.

"Squirtle squirtle!"

Ash spun around. It was the Squirtle Squad. Ash and his friends were surrounded.

Quickly, the Squirtle Squad wound thick ropes around Ash, Brock, and Misty. They picked up Pikachu and gently put it in a cage.

"Stop!" Ash cried.

But the Squirtle Squad didn't listen. They picked up the friends and carried them to a nearby cave.

Meowth popped out of the cave.

"You're not gonna *squirtle* out of this one!" Meowth said to Ash and his friends.

"Meowth?" Ash couldn't believe Team Rocket was behind this.

"I'm the Pokémon in charge here," Meowth said. "Just wait until my human pets get back."

"Don't believe him," Ash told the Squirtle Squad. "Meowth's a liar. Those humans aren't Meowth's pets. Team Rocket's trying to trick you into doing their dirty work for them."

"*Squirtle?*" the Squirtle leader asked.

"Don't listen to that human," Meowth said. "He's the liar."

Ash started to argue, but Brock stopped him.

"Ash, Pikachu's in bad shape," he said, nodding toward Pikachu's cage. "We have to heal Pikachu with Super Potion before it's too late. There's a shop in town that sells it."

Ash turned to the Squirtle leader. "Please! You've got to let me go into town. If I don't get some medicine, Pikachu will be in trouble."

"*Squirtle,*" the leader said flatly, shaking its head.

"Please trust me," Ash said. "As soon as I buy the medicine, I'll come back! I promise."

"*Squirtle squirtle,*" said the leader.

"Squirtle says that promises are cheap," Meowth translated.

Ash looked at Pikachu in the cage. Pikachu's eyes were still closed. It was barely breathing.

"I'm begging you," Ash said. "Please."

Ash was so worried, he began to cry. The Squirtle leader saw the tears fall down Ash's cheeks. The leader turned to Meowth.

"*Squirtle squirtle squirtle,*" the leader said.

Meowth sighed. "You can go. But Squirtle says if you're not back here by noon tomorrow, the redheaded girl's going to get her hair dyed purple!"

"Purple!" Misty shouted in rage. "Why you mangy little flea trap —"

But Ash was thrilled. The Squirtle Squad untied him.

"Don't worry Misty," Ash said. "I'll be back in a flash! I've got to do it for Pikachu."

Ash pulled his red cap down firmly on his head and ran down the road.

"It doesn't matter," Meowth muttered. "Even if that kid does make it back, we'll all be long gone!"

5

Race Against Time

Ash ran down the road to town. If he hurried, it should only take him a few hours to get to the Poké Mart.

Ash ran and ran. Soon daylight began to fade. Ash squinted into the setting sun. He thought he could see the rooftops of the town in the distance. He just had to cross that bridge up ahead, and he'd be close.

Almost there, Ash thought thankfully. *I'll get the Super Potion, and Pikachu will be cured.*

Ash jogged up to the bridge, then

stopped in his tracks. The rickety wooden bridge looked like it was made of toothpicks. Below was a 100-foot drop into the river.

Ash took a deep breath. He'd have to take it slow.

He set one foot on the bridge. The wood groaned, but it held fast.

Ash took another step. Then another.

"I can do this," Ash said, gaining confidence. "I can make it!"

Ash took another step.

The bridge splintered. Ash watched in horror as it cracked in two. Desperate, he grabbed onto one of the rails. But it was no use. The fragile piece broke, and Ash plummeted into the river below.

Splash! Ash landed safely in the deep water.

"Oh, man," Ash said. "That was close — ouch!"

Something was prodding him from behind.

A Goldeen!

"Hey!" Ash shouted. But he couldn't stop

Goldeen. The Water Pokémon pushed Ash down the river. The current was too strong for Ash to fight back.

Finally, the water was calm enough for Ash to swim away from Goldeen. He climbed wearily onto shore. He looked up. He could still see the town, but he was way off course.

Ash sighed, drained the water out of his hat, and continued on his way. He walked and walked and walked. When he finally reached town, the moon was shining brightly overhead.

"There's the market," Ash said, spotting a low building down the street. He ran up to the door and reached for the handle.

Then Ash collapsed, exhausted.

By the time he woke up, it was morning. Panicked, Ash sprang up and raced into the market.

Ash gasped. He had walked into the middle of a holdup!

Jessie and James were pointing ice guns at the customers in the store.

"Freeze!" Jessie shouted. "We want all the flash powder you've got!"

"And a large roll of dental floss," James added.

"What do you need them for?" the store clerk asked nervously.

Jessie sneered. "You want to get rid of the Squirtle Squad, don't you? The flash powder will scare them out of town."

"And the floss is for our teeth," James added.

The clerk handed over the flash powder and the floss. Jessie grabbed the goods, then shot off her ice gun.

"Farewell!" she yelled as she and James ran out.

Ash couldn't believe it. It was snowing inside the market, thanks to the ice gun.

Officer Jenny ran in.

"What happened here?" she asked.

Ash explained quickly. "We have to stop them," Ash said. "And I have to get that Super Potion to Pikachu before it's too late!"

"No problem," Jenny said. "I'll get you there."

Ash bought some Super Potion from the clerk, then followed Jenny outside. She hopped onto her motorcycle, and Ash jumped on behind her.

"Just hang on, Ash!" Jenny said.

The motorcycle sped down the road toward the cave. Ash had never traveled so fast before.

Then the motorcycle came to a screeching halt. Ash craned his neck to see what was the matter.

They were at the bridge. The same bridge that had collapsed under Ash yesterday.

"A dead end," Jenny said.

"It can't be," Ash said. "I've got to save Pikachu!"

Jenny revved up the motorcycle. "I think I know a way."

Jenny rode down a narrow road that ran along the mountain. After a few minutes, they came to an opening in the rock.

"Here's a secret entrance to the cave," Jenny said. "The passageway's too narrow for an adult to fit, but maybe you can squeeze through."

"I can do it!" Ash said. He stepped into the dark hole.

"Be careful!" Jenny called behind him.

Ash was in a tunnel of some kind. He groped his way along in the dark.

It wasn't long before he saw a light ahead.

The cave!

Ash ran toward the light. He climbed through the hole.

The cave was deserted. Ropes were scattered on the floor. And Pikachu's cage was empty!

"They're gone," Ash said in disbelief. "Pikachu!"

Ash rushed outside the cave. He saw the Squirtle Squad.

"I'm back by noon, just like I told you," Ash said. "What did you do with my friends?"

"We're right here," Misty said, stepping out from behind the Squad. "Where's the Super Potion for Pikachu?"

Ash pulled the potion out of his pocket. "I've got it," he said. He was so relieved to see Misty, Brock, and Pikachu. "So the Squirtle Squad didn't hurt you?"

"No way, Ash," Brock said. "They're not so bad. All they need is a good trainer."

Ash sprayed the Super Potion on

Pikachu. The Electric Pokémon's eyes fluttered open.

"Pikachu," Ash said. "Thank goodness."

But a loud blast shattered the peaceful silence. Black smoke filled the air.

"That blast," Ash said. "It's Team Rocket!"

As if on cue, Team Rocket's hot-air balloon appeared in the sky above them. Jessie and James hurled flash powder bombs at Ash and the Squirtle Squad.

Ash coughed. His eyes stung from the smoke. He could barely see.

"Meowth!" Jessie called out. "Carry Pikachu up the ladder!"

"No problem," Meowth said. James lowered Meowth to the ground on a rope ladder. Before Ash could stop it, Meowth scooped up Pikachu, who was still too weak to fight. James pulled the rope back into the balloon.

"Pikachu! No!" Ash yelled.

"So long, twerp," Jessie said. She threw another flash powder bomb at the cave.

The explosion started an avalanche of rock down the side of the mountain.

The rocks crashed down around them.

"Run for cover!" Ash shouted. "Into the cave!"

Squirtle Saves the Day

Misty and Brock helped lead the Squirtle Squad into the cave. Ash ran for the entrance, then stopped.

It was the Squirtle leader. The Pokémon was knocked out cold. It had been caught in the avalanche.

"Squirtle!" Ash cried. "Here I come!"

Ash dodged through falling rock to get to Squirtle's side.

"Are you okay?" Ash asked.

"Squirtle," Squirtle said weakly.

Another flash powder bomb whizzed

through the air. Ash threw himself over Squirtle's body to protect it.

The bomb exploded. More rocks tumbled down the mountain. But Ash was all right.

"*Squirtle!*" The Squirtle leader jumped up with determination. It looked stronger. Squirtle picked up Ash and ran back to the cave, to safety.

Another bomb fell. This one hit a nearby tree that caught on fire. More trees got caught in the blaze.

"This is fabulous," Jessie said. "First we tricked the Squirtle Squad into helping us. Now we'll get rid of them, and the town will call us heroes!"

But Ash wasn't going to let Team Rocket get away with their evil plan. He knew just what to do.

He turned to the Squirtle leader. "Squirtle! Water Gun Attack now!"

Squirtle nodded. It stepped out of the cave and aimed a powerful blast of water at Team Rocket's balloon. The balloon burst. Pikachu fell from Meowth's paws. Ash rushed out of the cave and caught Pikachu

as the hot-air balloon went spiraling off into the distance.

"Looks like Team Rocket's blasting off again!" the thieves cried as the balloon disappeared over the horizon.

"We did it!" Ash shouted.

"Team Rocket's gone," Brock said. "But now we've got that fire to deal with."

Ash looked. The fire had spread to the trees surrounding the mountain. It looked pretty bad.

At that moment, Officer Jenny pulled up on her motorcycle. "If this keeps burning, the whole town could go up in smoke!"

Ash had an idea. He turned to the Squirtle Squad. "If you work as a team, you can combine your water guns to put out the fire."

The Squirtle leader nodded. The Squirtle Squad worked together and fought the blaze with their Water Gun Attacks. Soon the fire was out.

"You did it!" Ash cried.

Officer Jenny called for backup. In minutes, some police cars pulled up. Ash and his friends got a ride into town, and so did the Squirtle Squad.

That night, the town gathered together for a celebration. Officer Jenny appointed the Squirtle Squad the town firefighters and gave them a special trophy.

"That was a happy ending," Ash said as he walked out of town with Misty, Brock, and Pikachu.

"It sure was," Misty said. "And I think it's going to get better. Look!"

Ash looked behind him. The Squirtle Squad leader was following them.

"*Squirtle squirtle,*" said the Water Pokémon.

"Would you like to come along with us?" Ash asked.

Squirtle nodded and took off its sunglasses. Then it ran up to Ash and jumped into his arms.

"Welcome to the team, Squirtle!" Ash said.

7

Tentacool and Tentacruel

Squirtle quickly became one of Ash's favorite Pokémon to use in battle. The small Pokémon packed a lot of power into its Water Gun, Bubble, and Hydro Pump Attacks. And because of its days with the Squirtle Squad, Squirtle worked well with Ash's other Pokémon. Squirtle was a real team player.

Squirtle and Pikachu became good friends. When Ash didn't need their help, they played games and had fun together. Pikachu always laughed at Squirtle's jokes.

But life on the road with Ash wasn't always fun and games.

Often, there was a lot of trouble.

Not long after Ash found Squirtle, he and his friends traveled to the island city of Porta Vista. While they were waiting for a boat to carry them off the island, they met a short woman with an angry face named Nastina. She wanted Ash to help her.

"There are a bunch of Tentacool in the ocean causing me problems," she said. "I'm trying to build a resort in the ocean off the island. It will be beautiful! It's surrounded by a coral reef. But the Tentacool keep destroying my boats and stopping my workers."

Nastina pointed. Ash looked out into the water. The steel beams of a half-built hotel gleamed in the sunlight.

"I need to finish my resort. I want you to exterminate the Tentacool for me," Nastina said. "I'll pay you a million dollars."

"A million!" Ash couldn't believe it. His eyes lit up.

Misty grabbed Ash by the sleeve. She pulled him away from Nastina. Brock and Pikachu followed.

"We don't need your money," Misty called back angrily.

"What was that all about?" Ash asked. "And what's a Tentacool, anyway?"

"Tentacool is a jellyfish Pokémon," Brock explained.

"Yeah," Misty said. "And it's cruel to kill them. If the Tentacool are hurting humans, there must be some reason for it."

"I guess you're right," Ash said.

"Pika! Pika!" Pikachu said suddenly.

Ash spun around. A white yacht came speeding up to the shore. And steering the yacht was Team Rocket!

"We'll get rid of those Tentacool for you," Jessie told Nastina.

Jessie and James lifted up a wooden barrel.

"We'll get rid of those jellyfish with our Super-Secret Stun Sauce!" James declared.

"Oh, no!" Misty cried.

Team Rocket laughed. Their boat roared out into the ocean.

Ash watched from the shore as Team Rocket got ready to spill the Super-Secret Stun Sauce into the ocean.

Suddenly, the water was filled with red, glowing light.

The Tentacool!

Ash had never seen these combination Water and Poison Pokémon before. The creatures looked like blue jellyfish with two long tentacles. Each had a red spot in the middle of its head, and two red spots on top. The glowing light was coming from the red spots.

Thousands and thousands of Tentacool surrounded Team Rocket's boat. They all beamed red light at the boat.

Boom! The boat exploded. Team Rocket flew off the boat and landed in the water.

The barrel holding the Super-Secret Stun Sauce broke apart. Slimy yellow liquid poured out and covered one of the Tentacool.

The Tentacool quivered. Glowing yellow light shone from its body.

Then the Tentacool grew.

And grew.

And grew.

Ash gasped. The tiny Tentacool was now ten stories tall. It had fourteen tentacles instead of two and two sharp stingers.

"It's evolved into a Tentacruel," Brock said. "But it's super-huge! Team Rocket's Stun Sauce must have caused it to grow."

"It doesn't matter what caused it," Ash said. "It's coming this way!"

Ash ran down the beach as Tentacruel climbed out of the water. Thousands of Tentacool followed it.

Tentacruel slid right to the center of town. It grabbed a tall building with its tentacles and crushed it like an egg.

The Tentacool followed it, breaking windows and crushing anything that stood in their way.

Then Tentacruel stopped. It spotted Meowth.

Tentacruel gripped Meowth with its ten-

tacles. A tentacle slid onto Meowth's head.

Meowth's eyes went blank. Then it began to talk in a zombielike voice.

"'We are Tentacool and Tentacruel. Hear us now,'" Meowth said.

"Tentacruel is using Meowth as a puppet," Brock said.

Meowth continued. "'You have destroyed our ocean home. Now we will destroy yours.'"

"Their home must be where that hotel is being built," Ash said.

"That's right!" Brock said. "The coral reef!"

The red spots on Tentacruel's head began to glow. A red beam shot out of them and hit another building, splitting it in two.

"I feel bad for Tentacruel," Misty said. "But we've got to stop it before somebody gets hurt."

"Right!" Ash said. "Time for a full power attack. Ready, Pikachu?"

Sparks flew from Pikachu's cheeks.

Ash took some Poké Balls from his belt. "Squirtle! Bulbasaur! Butterfree! Pidgeotto! Go!"

The Pokémon burst from their Poké Balls.

"Starmie! Staryu! Goldeen! Go!" Misty cried, throwing her Poké Balls.

Brock threw a Poké Ball, too. "Get ready, Zubat!" he yelled.

"All right, team," Ash said. "Get those Tentacool back into the sea!"

The Pokémon team sprang into action. Squirtle hopped on Zubat's back. Squirtle held on as Zubat flapped its wings and flew through the sky.

Pikachu jumped on Pidgeotto's back.

They lifted off and charged after the Tentacool.

Butterfree lifted up Bulbasaur and went after them.

Starmie, Staryu, and Goldeen took their position in the water.

The team started their assault with the Tentacool. Squirtle hit them with powerful water blasts. Bulbasaur lashed them with its Vine Whip. And Pikachu hit them all with one big electric shock.

The attack worked! The Tentacool scurried back into the water.

But the fight wasn't over.

Tentacruel came up behind the Pokémon team. It lashed out with its tentacles. Squirtle, Zubat, Butterfree, and Bulbasaur crashed to the ground.

But Pikachu and Pidgeotto stayed in the air near Tentacruel.

Then Tentacruel spoke through Meowth. "'Why are you taking the humans' side?'" it asked.

"Pikachu! Pika pika pi!" Pikachu replied.

"I think Pikachu is trying to reason with it," Brock remarked.

The Tentacruel was listening.

"Pikachu. Pika pi!" Pikachu said.

"Please listen," Misty said. "We humans won't destroy your home anymore."

"Pika pi," Pikachu said.

Tentacruel paused. Then it picked up Nastina with one tentacle.

Tentacruel spoke through Meowth. "'We will go. But if this happens again, we will not stop. Remember this well.'"

Nastina looked at the destroyed buildings around her. "Uh, okay," she said.

Tentacruel put down Nastina and

Meowth. Then it slid out into the ocean and swam away.

Pidgeotto landed on the ground. Pikachu jumped off its back and hugged Squirtle and the other Pokémon.

"Good work, guys," Ash said. "Together, we make a great team!"

8

Squirtle Power

Not only was Squirtle great at working with other Pokémon, but Squirtle also performed well in one-on-one battles.

Ash depended on Squirtle in battle after battle. And when Ash felt he was ready, he tried to get into the Pokémon League so that he could get closer to reaching his goal of being a Pokémon Master.

To join the Pokémon League, Ash had to battle five trainers and win.

The first trainer was a boy his age. The boy called on Exeggutor, a three-headed

coconut Pokémon. Ash used his Krabby, a Water Pokémon that looked like an orange crab. Krabby evolved dur-ing the battle and became a Kingler, which was stronger, with powerful claws that could cut through steel. Thanks to Kingler, Ash won the first battle easily. Kingler then went on to defeat the boy's Seadra and Golbat.

The next day, Ash faced his second opponent. This battle took place in a rock field in the mid-dle of the stadi-um. The regular battlefield was dotted with brown rocks and boulders. Ash knew this was so that the trainers could be tested under all types of conditions.

Ash stood at one end of the rock field and faced his opponent, a boy with brown hair who wore a blue vest. Pikachu stood at Ash's side.

"This is the second battle on the rock field," the announcer blared. "Each trainer can use only one more Pokémon. This choice will decide the battle. Which Pokémon will the competitors choose?"

The other trainer threw his red-and-white Poké Ball out over the field. The ball snapped open and a white light flashed. A pink Pokémon with a large horn on its forehead emerged from the light and landed on a boulder.

"A Nidorino!" the announcer said. "This Pokémon is known for its Poison Attacks. Which Pokémon will Ash use to fight Nidorino?"

Sparks flew from Pikachu's face. It had just defeated two of the boy's Pokémon and was ready to battle another. But Ash looked at Nidorino. It almost looked like a small dinosaur. Its body was all muscle. Ash knew he needed a Pokémon tough enough to absorb its strong attacks. But Pikachu was weak against Poison Types.

"Squirtle, I choose you!" Ash cried. He threw Squirtle's Poké Ball onto the field. Squirtle appeared, and flew through the air. It did a somersault and landed squarely on a boulder facing Nidorino.

"*Squirtle!*" it shouted. Its eyes gleamed, ready for the battle.

"I'm counting on you, Squirtle," Ash called out.

The Nidorino acted fast. It charged across the rock field at Squirtle.

"Nidorino has begun with a Tackle Attack," said the announcer.

Ash thought fast. "Squirtle! Withdraw!" he yelled.

Squirtle nodded. In a flash, it pulled its head, arms, and legs inside its hard shell.

Nidorino slammed into Squirtle head-on.

into Squirtle head-on. Squirtle's shell was knocked off the rock, but Squirtle was safe inside.

"Now roll!" Ash commanded.

Squirtle's shell rolled across the rock field. Nidorino chased after it. Squirtle rolled faster and faster. It rolled up the side of a large boulder, and then flew in the air.

"Now, Squirtle! Water Gun!" Ash ordered.

Squirtle popped out of its shell. It opened its mouth and shot a wide blast of water at Nidorino. The water sent Nidorino slamming back into a rock. The Pokémon was dazed, but not out. It rose to its feet and leaped in the air.

"End it with Skull Bash!" Ash yelled.

Squirtle changed its position so that its body formed a straight line. Then Squirtle lowered its head. A bright blue light glowed around Squirtle's head and upper body. Then Squirtle charged at Nidorino.

Slam! Squirtle crashed into Nidorino in midair.

"Squirtle's Skull Bash was right on!" the

announcer said. "It's taken a toll."

Nidorino thudded to the ground. Its eyes were closed, and it wasn't moving.

A judge walked out onto the field.

"Nidorino is incapable of battle," the judge said. "Ash wins the battle and this round of competition!"

The crowd cheered. Ash ran out onto the rock field and hugged Squirtle.

"Thanks, Squirtle," Ash said. "I knew I could count on you."

9

Wartortle

Squirtle was happy to help Ash win battles against other Pokémon trainers. Squirtle was always on call when Ash needed to fight off bad guys like Team Rocket. But Squirtle never forgot about its roots in the Squirtle Squad. If other Squirtle needed help, Ash's Squirtle was ready.

One day Ash's travels took him to a city on the ocean. Ash, Misty, Brock, and Pikachu walked down a sandy beach. Suddenly, a Water Pokémon crashed into them, knocking Ash down.

"Hey, why'd you do that?" Ash asked, brushing sand off his jeans. He studied the

Pokémon. It looked kind of like Squirtle, but it was dark blue and had long ears. It was taller than Squirtle, with a bigger tail.

"Wartortle. Tortle tortle," the Pokémon said. It sounded frantic.

"Wow. A Wartortle. Talk about your rare Pokémon," Brock remarked.

"A war-what-le?" Ash asked. He took out Dexter, his Pokédex.

"Wartortle, the turtle Pokémon," Dexter said. "The evolved form of Squirtle, its long, furry tail is a symbol of its age and wisdom."

"It doesn't look smart," Ash said. "It looks upset."

"Wartortle! Wartortle!" the Pokémon said.

"Pikachu, what's it saying?" Ash asked.

Usually Pikachu could understand what other Pokémon were saying. But Wartortle was talking too fast.

Pikachu took a Poké Ball from Ash's backpack. Squirtle appeared.

"Wartortle! Tortle tortle tortle!" the Wartortle told Squirtle. It pointed to the ocean.

"Squirtle! Squirtle squirtle," Squirtle replied.

Squirtle reached into its shell. It pulled

out a pair of sunglasses. Squirtle was ready for action.

"Hey! Squirtle Squad sunglasses!" Ash cried.

Squirtle put on the sunglasses. Then Squirtle and Wartortle ran down the beach, jumped in the water, and began to swim away.

"Squirtle, where are you going?" Ash called.

"There must be trouble," Brock said.

Ash ran down the beach. "Let's get a boat and follow them!"

10

Squirtle Island

"Follow that Squirtle!" Ash yelled.

A friendly fisherman lent the friends a boat. Misty called on her Water Pokémon Goldeen, Starmie, and Staryu to help pull the boat through the water.

Ash could see Squirtle and Wartortle in the distance, kicking up water as they swam through the waves.

"They're sure in a hurry," Ash remarked.

"Hey, Ash. Look!" Brock said. "There's an island ahead."

Ash squinted. A tiny island rose out of the water just up ahead. It didn't look like any island he had ever seen before. It looked like a Squirtle shell.

Brock was studying a map. "I can't find it anywhere on this map," he said. "That's strange."

"That must be where Squirtle and Wartortle are going," Misty said.

"Right!" Ash said. "Full speed ahead!"

A short while later, their boat reached the island's sandy shore. Squirtle and Wartortle were already there. The beach was covered with what looked like turtle shells.

"The beach is full of Squirtle and Wartortle," Brock said.

"But they're all inside their shells," Misty said. "I hope they're all right."

Brock knelt down by one of the shells. A low sound filled the air.

Snoring!

"It's okay," Brock said. "They're just sleeping."

"I don't get it," Ash said. Then he felt tugging on his sleeve. It was Squirtle and Wartortle. They pulled him down the beach.

In the center of the beach sat a large rock. A giant turtle shell rested on the rock. The shell was bigger than Ash.

"Wow!" Ash said. He took out Dexter.

"Blastoise, the shellfish Pokémon," Dexter said. "The evolved form of Wartortle, Blastoise's strength lies in its power rather than its speed. Its shell is like armor, and attacks from the hydro-cannon on its back are virtually unstoppable."

A Blastoise! Ash couldn't believe his luck. "I've got to get up close to it," he said.

Ash climbed up on the rock.

"It's either asleep or practicing its Withdraw Attack," Brock said.

Ash hugged the large shell. "I've waited such a long time to meet you, Blastoise," Ash said.

Suddenly, Ash began to feel tired. His eyelids drooped.

In seconds, his head was resting on the shell. Ash was sound asleep.

"Ash, are you all right?" Misty asked.

Concerned, Squirtle climbed up onto the rock. Squirtle tried to shake Ash awake. But then Squirtle's eyes started to close. Now Squirtle was asleep, too.

"Ash, wake up! Can you hear me?" Brock asked.

"Keep trying," Misty said.

"It's no good," Brock said. "He's out cold. It must have something to do with Blastoise."

Misty turned to Pikachu. "Try an Electroshock Alarm Clock!" she said.

Pikachu nodded. It closed its eyes. Sparks flew from its body as it charged up for the attack.

Boom! Pikachu aimed a bolt of electricity at Ash and Squirtle. It hit them, and they flew off Blastoise and landed on the beach. The charge shocked all of the Squirtle and Wartortle there.

Slowly, Ash opened his eyes. Around him, his Squirtle and all of the other

Squirtle and Wartortle were waking up and coming out of their shells.

"What's the matter, Ash? Dreaming about becoming a Pokémon Master?" Misty teased.

"I guess I did fall asleep," Ash said. "That's weird."

"And Squirtle dozed off right after you did," Brock said.

"I heard a sound coming from Blastoise just before I fell asleep," Ash said.

"What kind of sound?" Misty asked.

"Some kind of weird music. It sounded familiar," Ash replied. He turned to the Squirtle and Wartortle. "Did you hear the sound, too?"

They all nodded.

"This is creepy," Misty said and walked back toward the boat. "We'd better get off this island right away."

But Ash didn't move. "We're not going anywhere until we wake up that Blastoise."

Misty sighed. "I was afraid of that."

Ash turned to the group of Squirtle and Wartortle. "We won't be able to do it alone.

The Squirtle and Wartortle nodded and talked excitedly.

"All right!" Ash said. "Let Operation Wake-up begin!"

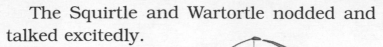

11

Kidnapped!

"Now let's see if I've got the story straight," Brock said after Ash's Squirtle translated for the other Squirtle and Wartortle.

"This island is the kingdom for turtle Pokémon. Blastoise is the turtle Pokémon king," Brock said.

The Squirtle and Wartortle nodded.

"A few days ago, Blastoise went to take a swim in the ocean," Brock continued. "But Blastoise didn't come home. You finally found Blastoise floating in the ocean, and when you dragged it ashore, you all fell asleep, too."

The group of turtle Pokémon nodded again.

Brock took a stethoscope from his bag and put it around his neck. He climbed up on the rock and held the stethoscope against Blastoise's shell.

"Be careful, Brock," Ash warned.

"I don't hear anything," Brock said. He frowned.

But then the shell began to rock. Two arms popped out. Then two legs. Then a large head.

Blastoise was awake!

"Blastoise," it said in a deep voice.

"What's it saying?" Ash asked.

Ash's Squirtle approached Blastoise. *"Squirtle? Squirtle squirtle?"* it asked.

"Blastoise," Blastoise replied. It pointed to the water cannon on its shoulder. Brock stepped up to the cannon. Something was stuck inside. It looked pink, and kind of round.

"What is this thing?" Brock asked.

Squirtle climbed up next to the cannon. It poked the pink blob.

The blob moved. A pink ear popped out of the cannon's mouth. Then another.

A strange sound began to fill the air. It sounded like a song.

"Oh, no," Misty said. "I hope it's not what I think it is."

The song got louder. Ash knew that song. It sounded like a lullaby.

"Jigglypuff!" Ash cried.

"That's it!" Brock said. "Jigglypuff loves

to sing. But its song puts humans and Pokémon to sleep. Jigglypuff must have gotten stuck in Blastoise's cannon. Then it —" Brock couldn't finish. He yawned.

"Oh, no," Ash said sleepily. He couldn't keep his eyes open.

All around him, Squirtle and Wartortle were retreating into their shells. Ash sank down into the sand.

Everyone on the island was fast asleep.

Just then, Team Rocket approached the island in a submarine shaped like a Gyarados — a Water Pokémon that resembled a sea monster. They brought the submarine above water. Then Jessie, James, and Meowth looked at the beach through binoculars.

"We'll grab your Pokémon in a snap . . . " Jessie said.

" . . . before you wake up from your little nap!" finished James.

Jessie and James walked up to the head of the Gyarados that was carved into the ship's bow. Stuffed in the Gyarados' mouth was a giant suction cup attached to a pole. The pole was attached to a long rope.

"With this device, grabbing Blastoise should be a breeze!" Jessie said.

Meowth also hopped up next to the Gyarados head. "Let's do it!"

Meowth pulled a switch next to the head. The suction-cup arrow flew across the water, across the beach, and stuck right onto Blastoise's shell.

"Now let's reel in our catch," said Meowth, who grabbed onto a handle and began to reel in the rope. The rope pulled

Blastoise off the rock, across the beach, and into the water.

"This is too easy," James remarked.

Working together, Team Rocket pulled the heavy shell onto the deck. Then they hauled it down into the hull of the submarine.

"Our boss will be so pleased with Blastoise," Jessie said.

"Just wait," James said. "Now we can go back and get all of those other Pokémon!"

Meanwhile, Ash and his friends were waking up on the beach. So were the other Pokémon.

A cry of panic rose up as everyone realized that Blastoise was missing from the rock.

"Squirtle! Squirtle!"

"Wartortle! Wartortle!"

The Water Pokémon didn't know what to do.

But Ash's Squirtle remained calm. It shot a forceful stream of water at the other Squirtle and Wartortle. That got their attention.

Squirtle jumped up on Blastoise's rock.

"*Squirtle! Squirtle! Squirtle!*" Squirtle cried.

The Squirtle and Wartortle cheered. Then Ash's Squirtle ran down the beach with Pikachu at its side. All the other Squirtle and Wartortle followed.

"Wow, Ash, your Squirtle is a real leader," Misty said.

"Well, that's what happens when you've got a great trainer," Ash bragged.

"Or maybe they're just impressed by the sunglasses," Brock said.

Ash frowned. "Let's follow them. They must be looking for Blastoise."

It wasn't long before Squirtle and Pikachu found the trail left in the sand when Blastoise's shell was dragged away. The trail led to the water's edge.

All of the Pokémon looked out into the ocean. Then Pikachu pointed.

"Pika!" it shouted.

Ash looked. There was some kind of boat or submarine in the water. It was shaped like a Gyarados.

"That's got to be Team Rocket," Misty said. "Who else would do something like this?"

"Right!" Ash said. "Squirtle, you know what to do."

Squirtle nodded. Then it dove into the waves. The other Squirtle and Wartortle followed.

"You can do it, Squirtle!" Ash called after them.

"I hope so," Misty said. "Or we'll never see Blastoise again!"

Blastoise in Action

Inside the Gyarados submarine, Team Rocket was very pleased with themselves.

"The Boss will give me a big reward for this," Jessie said, greedily eyeing the Blastoise shell.

"You? What about me?" James protested.

"Of course, this whole thing was my idea," Meowth said.

"Your idea?" Jessie said angrily. She aimed a kick at Meowth.

Jessie missed. She kicked a hole in the

wall of the submarine instead. Water began to pour into the hull.

"Now look what you've done," James snapped.

"It's all Meowth's fault!" Jessie said.

The three Pokémon thieves glared at one another.

Then their eyes began to droop.

Jessie yawned. "Something strange is happening. I feel so —"

Jessie, James, and Meowth dropped to the floor. Jigglypuff's song had put them to sleep.

Water was pouring through the submarine now.

The sub was sinking!

Outside the submarine, the Squirtle and Wartortle were hard at work. They swam around the sub, surrounding it. They struggled to keep the sinking sub afloat. With all their might, they pushed the submarine through the water and back onto the beach.

The submarine crashed into the sand. Blastoise's shell flew out of the opening and landed safely on the beach.

The cold water woke up Team Rocket. They climbed out onto the deck of the submarine.

Jessie glared at Ash, Misty, and Brock.

"What kind of trick are you pulling?" she asked. "How did we get here?"

"Don't give us any attitude," Misty answered right back. "These Squirtle and Wartortle just saved your lives."

"Yeah," Ash said. "Just get out of here."

Jessie sneered. "We're not going anywhere without our Blastoise."

"That's right!" James said. "Time for Plan B."

Jessie, James, and Meowth disappeared inside the submarine.

"What are they up to?" Ash wondered.

Four wheels appeared on the submarine. The Gyarados started to roll across the beach.

"That Gyarados sub is doing double duty as a tank!" Ash realized.

Two tiny windows on the tank opened up, and two metal arms extended from the windows. Each arm had a grabbing hand on the end.

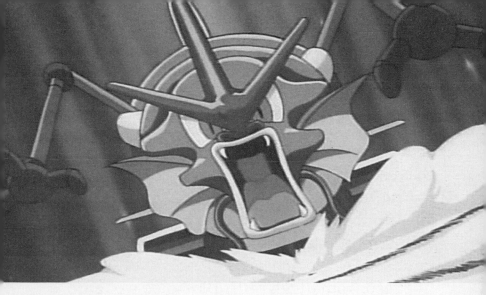

The Squirtle and Wartortle faced the tank. They shot hard blasts of water at it.

But they couldn't stop it. The arms grabbed them one by one and tossed them to the side.

"We've got to do something to save them," Brock said.

Ash had an idea. "Squirtle! Pikachu!" he called.

The two Pokémon ran up to him.

"Use your attacks to wake up Blastoise," Ash said. "Blastoise is big enough to stop that thing."

Squirtle and Pikachu nodded and faced the large shell.

Squirtle shot a stream of water from its mouth. Then Pikachu aimed an electric charge into the stream.

The water carried the electric charge, giving it extra power. When the charge hit Blastoise, it rocked the shell.

The shock knocked the Jigglypuff loose. The pink Pokémon flew out of the water cannon and landed inside the Gyarados tank.

Freed from Jigglypuff, Blastoise woke up again. Its head, arms, and legs emerged from its shell.

"Blastoise! Stop that tank!" Ash shouted. "The Squirtle and Wartortle need your help."

Blastoise stomped across the beach. It faced the Gyarados tank.

The tank charged at Blastoise, but Blastoise held out its hands.

It stopped the tank in its tracks.

Then the mechanical arms tried to grab Blastoise. Blastoise took one in each hand and crushed them as if they were twigs.

Finally, Blastoise aimed its water can-

nons at the tank. Two massive waves of water hit the tank full force.

The Squirtle and Wartortle joined in. They all aimed water attacks at the Gyarados tank.

The water blasts pushed the tank down the beach and back into the water. The mangled tank bobbed in the waves, then it slowly started to sink.

"All right!" Ash said. "We did it. Great work, everybody!"

"It isn't over yet," Misty said. "Jigglypuff is trapped inside that thing!"

13

Squirtle Saves the Day — Again

"Squirtle! Squirtle!" Ash's Squirtle cried.

Squirtle jumped into the water. It swam toward the sub as fast as it could.

Ash watched anxiously as Squirtle approached the submarine. Billows of black smoke rose from the ship. It looked like it might be on fire.

"Squirtle! Be careful!" Ash called out.

Suddenly, a loud explosion rocked the

beach. Ash watched in horror as the submarine blew apart in a fiery blast.

"No!" Ash cried.

Black smoke filled the air. Ash couldn't see a thing.

Then the smoke cleared.

Ash saw Team Rocket flying through the air, far away from the beach.

Then he saw something else.

Squirtle!

Squirtle was swimming through the water. Jigglypuff sat on its back.

Exhausted, Squirtle swam onto the beach. Jigglypuff jumped off and smiled.

Ash hugged Squirtle and lifted it into the air. "Squirtle? Are you okay?"

Squirtle nodded.

"What about you, Jigglypuff?" Misty asked.

Jigglypuff smiled. Then it pulled out a microphone.

"Jigglypuff, no!" Misty cried.

But it was too late. Jigglypuff began to sing its lullaby. In seconds, every human and Pokémon on the beach was snoring peacefully.

Jigglypuff frowned. No one would ever hear it finish its song!

Angry, Jigglypuff held up a black Magic Marker. It hopped along the beach, drawing shapes on the shells of the turtle Pokémon and marking up the faces of Ash and his friends.

Then Jigglypuff hopped away.

A few hours later, everyone woke up.

"Not again," Misty groaned, looking around at the black marks on everyone. "This stuff is so hard to wash off!"

"It doesn't matter," Ash said. "I'm just glad everything worked out."

"That's right," Brock said. "We did a lot today. We figured out the mystery of the sleeping Blastoise. And we kept Team Rocket from stealing all these Pokémon."

"Squirtle's the real hero," Ash said. "Squirtle led all the other Squirtle and Wartortle to save Blastoise. And Squirtle rescued Jigglypuff."

"*Squirtle. Squirtle squirtle,*" Squirtle said.

"What's it saying, Pikachu?" Ash asked.

"*Pika pika pi,*" Pikachu said.

Ash smiled. "Squirtle said it's proud to be a part of our team!"

Proud to be a part of our team. The memory of the adventure on the island with the turtle Pokémon drifted through Ash's mind as he lounged on the bank of the stream, his eyes closed.

I'm proud of Squirtle, too, Ash thought. *Misty was right. Squirtle is one of my best Pokémon.*

Splash!

A blast of cold water roused Ash from his daydream.

"Not again!" Ash sat up. Squirtle sat in the stream, laughing.

Ash smiled at Squirtle.

Squirtle was never going to change. Ash knew it was always going to play practical jokes. But he also knew that Squirtle would always be there for him when he needed it.

"That's my Squirtle!" he said.

About the Author

Tracey West has been writing books for more than ten years. When she's not playing the blue version of the Pokémon game (she started with a Squirtle), she enjoys reading comic books, watching cartoons, and taking long walks in the woods (looking for wild Pokémon). She lives in a small town in New York with her family and pets.

HEY, KIDS!

ENTER THE PIKACHU PEEKABOO CONTEST!

Count the number of times you see this Pikachu image in this book and enter to win valuable Pokémon Prizes.

Official Rules:

1. NO PURCHASE NECESSARY. To enter, complete this official entry coupon or hand print your name, address, birth date, and telephone number, and answer to the contest question on a 3" x 5" card and mail by 6/1/00 to: PIKACHU PEEKABOO! Contest, c/o Scholastic Inc., P.O. Box 7500, Jefferson City, MO 65101.

2. Contest open to residents of the USA no older than 15 as of 12/31/00, except employees of Scholastic Inc., its respective affiliates, subsidiaries, respective advertising, promotion, and fulfillment agencies, and immediate families. Contest is void where prohibited by law.

3. Except where prohibited, by accepting the prize, winner consents to the use of his/her name, age, entry, and/or likeness by sponsors for publicity purposes without further notice or compensation.

4. Winners will be judged by Scholastic Inc., whose decision is final, based on their answers. Only one prize per winner. All winners will be selected on or about 6/15/00, by Scholastic Inc., whose decision is final. Odds of winning are dependent on the number of entries received. Winners and their legal guardians will be required to sign and return an affidavit of eligibility and liability release within 14 days of notification, or the prize will be forfeited.

5. Prizes: **Grand Prize:** A set of Pokémon video games. (Estimated retail value: $200) **1st Prize:** 25 First Prize winners will receive a Pokémon home video. (Estimated retail value: $25). **2nd Prize:** 50 Second Prize winners will receive a Pokémon bag. (Estimated retail value $20). **3rd Prize:** 100 Third Prize winners will receive a Pokémon key chain. (Estimated retail value: $10) No substitution or transfer of prize allowed, except by sponsor due to prize unavailability.

6. Prizes are non-transferable, not returnable, and cannot be sold or redeemed for cash. No substitutions allowed. Taxes on prizes are the responsibility of the winner. By accepting the prize, winner agrees that Scholastic Inc. and its respective officers, directors, agents, and employees will have no liability or responsibility for any injuries, losses, or damages of any kind resulting from the acceptance, possession, or use of any prize and they will be held harmless against any claims of liability arising directly or indirectly from the prizes awarded.

7. For list of winners, send a self-addressed stamped envelope after 6/15/00 to: PIKACHU PEEKABOO! Contest WINNERS, c/o Scholastic Inc., P.O. Box 7500, 2931 East McCarty Street, Jefferson City, MO 64102.

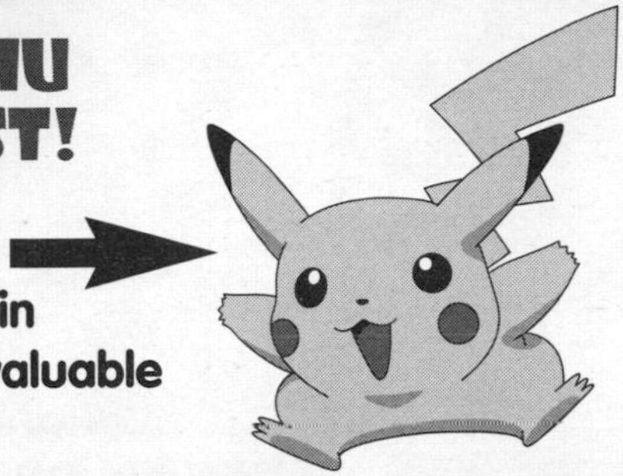

CONTEST QUESTION

How many times does the Pikachu shown above appear in this book?________

Name________________________________ Birth date________________

Address____

City________________________________ State__________ Zip__________

POKc200